Graham Denton is a writer, anthologist and passionate promoter of poetry for children. He lives in East Yorkshire with his wife and two children. Graham claims to be unsuperstitious, but definitely believes it is very bad luck to go shopping on a Saturday afternoon, especially when there is live football on the television (at least, that's what he tells his wife).

Jane Eccles loves black cats, ignores magpies and isn't bothered about the number thirteen or putting shoes on the table. She has neither found a four-leaf clover nor owned a lucky rabbit's foot. In fact, she's not superstitious at all, touch wood.

Also published by Macmillan

How to Survive School
Poems chosen by David Harmer

How to Embarrass Teachers
Poems chosen by Paul Cookson

Can We Have Our Ball Back, Please?
Football poems by Gareth Owen

Silly Superstitions

Poems chosen
by Graham Denton

Illustrated
by Jane Eccles

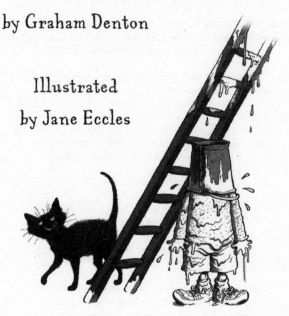

MACMILLAN CHILDREN'S BOOKS

For Dianna, Catherine and Frankie, and in memory of
Christopher Earp (1989–2006) GD

First published 2006 by Macmillan Children's Books
a division of Macmillan Publishers Limited
20 New Wharf Road, London N1 9RR
Basingstoke and Oxford
www.panmacmillan.com

Associated companies throughout the world

ISBN: 978-0-330-43727-1

3 5 7 9 8 6 4 2

A CIP catalogue record for this book is available from
the British Library.

Typeset by Tony Fleetwood
Printed and bound in Great Britain by Mackays of Chatham plc, Kent

Contents

The Door

With apologies to Miroslav Holub!

Do not open the door!
Maybe inside there is
a seething cauldron,
a wild-tailed dragon,
or a teacher's eye, staring . . .

Do not open the door!
Maybe a snake slithers,
four walls
like an invisible clock
tick away
a never-ending morning.

A teacher's tongue
wags in the darkness
with *your* name on it . . .

Do not open the door!
Maybe the ghost of Voldemort
lurks in the shadows,
waiting . . .

Do not open the door!
Maybe
through the breathing darkness
a gnarled, insistent finger
silently unfurls to point
to someone . . .

It
has chosen

YOU!

Judith Nicholls

At the House of Superstition

There's a crack in the mirror,
An open umbrella,
A table laid for thirteen,
And the grass on the lawn
All shaven and shorn
Is a sinister arsenic green.

There's a ladder that leans
At an angle which means
Pass beneath and there's trouble in store!
And a black cat asleep,
And no one to sweep
The salt that lies spilt on the floor.

There's a terminal look
To the Visitors' Book,
No radio, TV or phone,
And today and tomorrow
Are both born to sorrow
Like the magpie which flies off alone.

John Mole

First Things

As I walk on to the pitch
Before the game starts
I kiss the turf
Face north, east, south and west
Do a Russian sword dance
Touch my knees with my chin
Touch the goalposts at both ends
Bounce the ball three times on my head
Whistle 'England's Coming Home'
Secretly touch my lucky underpants
(That have never been washed)
And when I've done those things
I know that we will always
And without fail
WIN

Sometimes.

Roger Stevens

Unlucky Uncle Eric

Unlucky Uncle Eric
While one day playing cricket
Saw a four-leaf clover
And thought that he would pick it.
As he bent down towards the ground
To pluck the lucky leaf,
The cricket ball flew through the air
And knocked out all his teeth.
He shouted, 'Drat!' and dropped the bat,
Which landed on his toes.
It bounced back up and cracked his chin,
Then smacked him in the nose.
Smeared in blood and caked in mud,
He said, 'I'm glad that's over.'
Then, with a sigh, he held up high
His lucky four-leaf clover.

Gervase Phinn

Lucky Lou

Lucky Lou was luckier
than anyone the world over.
Lou had ninety rabbits' feet,
his lawn was made of four-leafed clover.

Lou had lots of lucky bracelets
all adorned with lucky charms;
some he wore around his ankles,
others jingled on his arms.

Lou would keep his lucky hat on
even while he took a bath.
Black cats always walked behind him
so they wouldn't cross his path.

Never walked beneath a ladder.
Never wore a stitch of black.
Never broke a single mirror.
Never stepped upon a crack.

Lucky Lou was luckier
than anyone else, it's said.
Till the day that grand piano
fell and landed on his head.

Kenn Nesbitt

How Superstitions Were Made

As the witches got fed up with burning alive
They held a big conference in 1605
To talk about things like ducking stools
'Quite frankly these people must take us for fools'
'They really are getting too big for their shoes'
'It's time someone taught them to pay us our dues!'
'Too long we have aided the sick and the weak
See how they repay us, they say we are *freaks*!'

So they mixed up a potion, a terrible brew
With horrible things in, the way witches do
'Let's throw in some ghosties for spookish fun
We'll scare them all silly before we are done!'
Add the usual collection of toads, newts and bats
Wolf's bane and slugs and the insides of rats
Stir in old wives' tales (some young ones too)
A curse for good measure to thicken the brew
The whole recipe just appealed to those witches
They stirred and they danced and they cackled in stitches.

So now the poor mortals caught under the spell
Would be frightened at night-time *and* daytime as well
They won't walk under ladders or pass on the stairs
And no longer live life without any cares
They'll cross their fingers – just in case
That silly scaredy human race.

And so for this evil they invented a word
Which covers all fears from bad to absurd
And this is how the *Stishuns* were made
Then they became *Super* within a decade.

Barbara Beveridge

Luck of the Irish (1912)

Lucky Seamus finds a four-leaf clover.
Lucky Seamus strokes a big black cat:
hits upon a horseshoe – his smile grows –
feels a money spider on his nose . . .

From a distant uncle,
inherits *stylish* clothes.
There, in a secret pocket,
one long-forgotten locket!

Lucky Seamus sells it:
holding folding,
strolls to town;
spins half a crown,
puts it down
and wins the local lottery.

A third-class ticket
his hot property,
'Sure and it'll be so romantic
to be crossing the gigantic Atlantic.'

Yes, here lucky Seamus stands,

on board the *Titanic*.

Mike Johnson

Crewless Clueless

In the sea-shanty seas, beneath rock 'n' roll waves,
Dance horn-piping bones in their seaweedy graves.
Where terrible teeth flash a sharp, sharky grin
And snigger at pirates who won't learn to swim.
They think it's unlucky, they say, 'Flippin' heck!
If we learned how to swim, bet your boots we'd be
wrecked!
Swimming's for lubbers who live on dry ground;
If pirates could swim then we'd surely be drowned.'

But daft Captain Clueless was sick as a chip
Every time that a pirate fell out of his ship.
'Well, pluck my best parrot! Oh, what a to-do!
If any more drown I'll have lost all my crew!'
There was Hooligan Henry out walking the plank –
He stepped off the end and unfortunately sank.
That poser Sam Swanky had swashed his last buckle
When he fell off the poop and ended up scuttled.

One-arm Ed, Toothless Fred, Nasty Ned and Scarface,
Then poor Splat the parrot all sank without trace.
'Well, jiggle my peg leg!' the daft captain said.
'I'd keel-haul the lot but they're already dead.
If you swabbies keep falling off into the drink
I'll have to start thinking unthinkable thinks.
The sea's full of water, right up to the brim,
Unlucky or not, you must learn how to swim!'

So, in cute swimming cozzies and feeling like prats,
They swapped skull and crossbones for matching swim hats
And putting on armbands to help them to float
They all held their noses and jumped off the boat.
'Well, gargle my grog! You lads should have waited.
Don't armbands work better if they are inflated?'
Through the shaggy green seaweed float sea-shanty songs,
It's the sound of drowned pirates – they were right all along!

Maureen Haselhurst

Volunteer

Well some poem's got to do it . . .
step forward to be counted,
show what it's made of,
stand up for what it believes –
so why not me?

Call me rash,
call me brave,
call me generous . . .
a poem's got to do what a poem's got to do –
and anyway
it's only a load of superstitious mumbo-jumbo
so I'm volunteering.
Put *me* on page thirteen!

Philip Waddell

The Old Cures

To cure children of bed-wetting
They gave them for a feed
Roast mouse on toast (including fur):
Good results guaranteed.
For whooping cough, take nine fat frogs
And boil them into soup:
A few lip-smacking bowls of that
Very soon relieved the whoop.
For burns, just lick a lizard
To ease the pain and sting.
Nosebleeds? Toads in vinegar
Were thought to be the thing.

For fevers, throw live spiders
Into water – two or three.
When they curl up into balls –
Drink down the remedy!

Did these old cures really work?
(They're all true, I vow!)
Or were they worse than being ill?
Just give thanks you're living *now*!

Eric Finney

An Apple a Day Keeps the Doctor Away

I have a bag of apples
which I keep just near the bed,
and when the doctor rings the bell
I pelt one at his head!

Geoff Lowe

A Model Life

Mr Vernon Potato of Netherton-Willow
Slept on a clover-stuffed, horseshoe-shaped pillow.
When laying the table he never crossed knives,
His black cat, Matilda, had forty-nine lives.
He kept his umbrella tight-folded indoors,
And his lucky white rabbit had four lucky paws.
When storms came he never stood under a tree,
So he lived to one hundred and seventy-three.

Petonelle Archer

Mrs McQueen

She keeps a pet peacock
to chase off black cats;
she walks under ladders,
steps on all cracks.

She opens her brolly
inside the front door;
she won't cross her fingers,
says it's a bore!

Her mirror is crazed
as an egg in a cup;
on her door hangs a horseshoe –
bottom-side up.

Her vases are filled
with sweet-smelling may
and six peacock feathers
stare from her bay.

She throws away wishbones,
won't have mistletoe,
buys lucky mince pies –
to feed her pet crow.

Born on a Friday,
one dark Halloween,
she moved on St Swithin's,
dressed all in green.

She's all right *so* far
from what I have seen –
but *I* would touch wood
if I lived at Thirteen!

Judith Nicholls

Seven Unlucky Thirteens

*A Thirteen: a three-line poem with thirteen syllables in a
4-5-4 pattern*

Threw a black cat
Over my shoulder
Broke a mirror

Not so lucky
Horseshoe broke my toes
Still on the horse

Walked round ladder
Dislocated hip
Tripped on black cat

Friday thirteenth
Full moon, Halloween
Midnight . . . who's there?

Stuck inside house
New umbrella up
Won't fit through door

Whoops! Seven years.
Should not have broken
Mirror on dad

White rabbit's foot
In my coat pocket . . .
Rabbit not pleased

Paul Cookson

Desperation

I tried everything I could . . .
    wished on a star
    and a four-leaf clover
    knocked on wood
    rubbed a rabbit's foot
    kept dice in my pocket
    wore my pants inside out
    my cap back to front
    shoes on the wrong feet . . .

nothing worked,
my luck ran out.

'*Right*,' said Dad.
'*Where's your school report?*'

Patricia Leighton

A Sad Ending

A cynical man from Mauritius
Thought it foolish to be superstitious
When a black cat passed near
He stood firm, without fear
(What a shame that the panther was vicious).

Rachel Rooney

One for Sorrow, Two for Joy

On the day I decided
I really wasn't going to be
Superstitious any more
I disturbed a magpie in a tree
As I ran around the field,
So I forced myself to go
Round again
To make sure I saw another one.
But when I did
I worried that it was
The same one as before.

Chris Eddershaw

The Scottish Play

(A theatrical superstition)

You may speak of ghosts and witches,
You may tell (beneath your breath)
A tale of blood and daggers,
Of ghastly dreams and death,
You may even mention murder

     BUT

Don't EVER say Macb . . .

Clare Bevan

Castle Calamity

It has long been believed that spilling salt at table brings bad luck, which can only be avoided by tossing a pinch of salt over a shoulder – sometimes.

The baron Lord Punchup strode into the hall,
invited to dine by his neighbour.
The Earl of Muchcarping had promised a feast –
the result of great planning and labour.

Boars' heads, jellied trotters and soft griddled eggs
were eagerly scoffed by the plateful.
Lord Punchup grew jovial, quaffing the mead,
and his attitude mellowed less hateful.

For he and the earl had been warring for years.
Now surely the feuding could end.
'I hope,' said the earl with an amiable smile,
'henceforward you'll count me your friend.'

The baron responded with multiple nods
and slapped a huge hand on his belly.
'Most certainly, sir!' he declared, and he laughed
with his beard shedding droplets of jelly.

While everyone cheered and their goblets were raised
the son of the earl, near his daddy,
reached out for some nuts and knocked over the salt.
(What a cumbersome weed of a laddie!)

His mother, the countess, drew in a sharp breath.
'I'm ever so sorry,' he told her.
She snapped: 'It's bad luck, boy, to leave it a-lying.
Be quick! Throw it over your shoulder.'

With careless abandon the son of the earl
did exactly what Mummy had said.
But sadly Lord Punchup was hit in the face
and the salt showered over his head.

The baron arose with a thunderous roar.
(All feasting and quaffing had halted.)
'I came to this castle with peaceful intent,'
he declared, 'but I've just been a-salted.'*

With unsteady steps (and a gash on his nose),
he staggered his way to the door.
Then turning, he pointed his sword at the earl.
'This means, sir, we're now back at war!'

Then loudly the countess berated her son.
'You stupid, calamitous clot!
When telling you, "Quick, throw it over your shoulder,"
I meant only *salt*, not the *pot*.'

Barry Buckingham

* This should be spelled 'assaulted', of course,
but that wouldn't be so funny.

Reverse Curse

Me mother's daft, me mother's mad
and shall I tell you why?
She's put her shirt on inside out.
It's true, I wouldn't lie.

She said, until she goes to bed
she'll wear the shirt this way
for something bad will happen
if she changes it today.

'But everyone will laugh,' I sneer,
'That's bad enough. What's worse?'
She said that she could crash the car,
or trip, or lose her purse.

'Of all the superstitious rot!'
declared my Auntie Mabel –
'She just wants to show the world
her shirt's designer label.'

Celia Gentles

Smelly Pants

I love to wear my lucky pants
They're really rather posh
But it's been six weeks so I think it's time
To put them in the wash.

Jane Saddler

All the Same...

S illy
Unbelievable
P oppycock.
E yewash.
R ubbish.
S oft-headed
T osh.
I ncredible
T waddle.
I rrational
Old wives' tales.
Nonsensical
S care stories.

Philip Waddell

It's Friday the 13th
Tomorrow

It's Friday the 13th tomorrow.
A black cat just leaped in my path.
I'm not superstitious, but this might
explain why I'm failing in math.

By chance I walked under a ladder
a teacher had placed by the wall.
In class my umbrella popped open,
and that's why I tripped in the hall.

The salt spilt this morning at breakfast.
While walking I stepped on a crack.
I took off my shoes on the table.
It looks like my future is black.

This evening I busted a mirror,
which means that the next seven years
are due to be filled with misfortune,
catastrophes, mishaps and tears.

With all the bad luck I'm confronting,
it seems that I'm probably cursed.
It may be the 13th tomorrow,
but Thursday the 12th is the worst.

Kenn Nesbitt

Just a Coincidence

Did you know
witches meet in twelves
(and the devil makes thirteen),
and they always meet
on Fridays?
Friday . . . thirteen.
Get it?

And do you know what?
Our school's got twelve staff
(plus the Head).
And staff meetings
are always
. . . on a Friday!
Weird or what?

Patricia Leighton

A Date with Fate

Written on the tombstone of a girl named May
who died on June 1st

Dear May lies here –
she lived in fear
of perishing
this very day.

I guess she knew
the first of June
would prove to be
the end of May!

Graham Denton

Trick or Treat?

At the house on the hill
We were scared but I said,
'Well, I will if you come too.'
So we knocked at the door
Where the cats stalked all day
With their green eyes ablaze
And their fur in a frosty blue haze . . .

The door was unlocked
And opened halfway
By a lady in grey
And a red fur-trimmed gown,
Who smiled – with a frown –
As she looked in my eyes
With a gaze cold and wise.

I gulped and I said,
'Trick or treat?'
And she reached out a hand
And she gave me a sweet
And she quietly said:
'Do not eat this sweet till the morn
Till the darkness is gone!'
And closed the door with a smile.

But, in a while, we forgot
What she warned as she
Gave us the sweet when
We said, 'Trick or treat?'
And later that night
By the light of the moon
I recalled what she told me
As I swallowed the sweet
Several hours too soon . . .

Now on the street
On the hill, by the door
There is one more
Little black cat
Listening for steps
And waiting for scraps
In the cold . . .

Trevor Millum

Getting a Little Hairy

There once was a werewolf from Trace
Who said, 'It is such a disgrace
    How the townspeople run
    And become so undone
By these few little hairs on my face.'

Robert Scotellaro

Old Country Warning

Never let a rabbit eat your socks;
Foul fortune comes to those who do.
If a rabbit looks suspicious
Let him know you could get vicious
Raise your fist at him and holler SHOO!

Never let a rabbit eat your socks;
For if you do you will be cruelly cursed.
But if you can't avoid it
(And sometimes you can't, I've tried it)
Do make sure you take your feet out first.

Frances Nagle

Omen Road

A black cat ran across my path,
an owl began to hoot.
A magpie landed on the grass.
I threw him a salute.
I hurried down the Omen Road
avoiding every crack.
The cat miaowed, the magpie crowed.
I didn't dare glance back.

I met a lady in the street
in tatty cut-off jeans,
with sapphire slippers on her feet
and socks of forest green.
I said, 'You can't wear blue and green,
it really isn't right.'
She howled, 'Beware! Beware thirteen,
it's Halloween tonight.'

I caught the number-thirteen bus
and chatted with the driver.
He told me that I really must
not ever kill a spider.
I said, 'I'm vegetarian
and don't eat fish or meat.'
He said, 'Well, I'm a caring man
and don't wear rabbit's feet.'

We talked about the weather,
the world, and how his wives
each wore a peacock feather
and dared to cross their knives.
He tossed salt past my shoulder.
Again a magpie crowed.
That's when we hit the boulder
and plunged off Omen Road.

Celia Gentles

Several Sensible Superstitions

It is unlucky to forget the date of your own birthday.

It is *slightly* unlucky to wear your black T-shirt while brushing your teeth.

It is *very* unlucky to walk under a ladder when a window-cleaner is falling from it.

Always smile at dentists: this is *very* lucky indeed.

It is *sometimes* lucky to smile at teachers; but at other times they just wonder what evil tricks you are planning, in which case it is unlucky.

It is unlucky to eat glass or to swallow a *whole* tree, and it is *doubly* unlucky to swallow a whole tree made of glass.

When breathing in and out, it is *very* unlucky to do lots of one and none of the other.

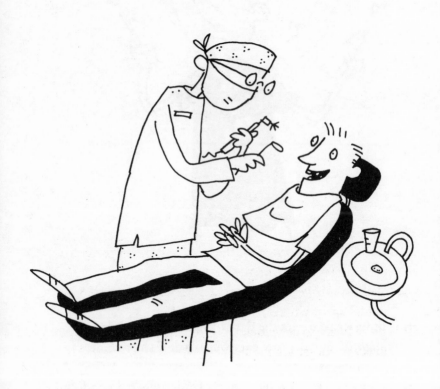

chomp chomp!

It is *quite* unlucky to step on the cracks in the pavement if
    they are large enough to fall down.
At funerals, it is *very, very* bad luck to wear brown clothes
    made out of wood.
It is *quite* lucky to remember this list, but it is *nearly* as
    lucky to forget it completely.

David Bateman

Some Very Sensible Superstitions

If you spit
into the wind
three times
you'll get a very
wet face.

A black cat
crossing your path
means
it's going
in a different direction
to you.

Keep
a piece of coal
in your pocket
and you'll always have
a dirty handkerchief.

If you say
the same thing as your friend
at the same time
one of you
should shut up.

Find
a four-leaf clover
in the evening and
you were unlucky
not to find it
earlier.

If you walk to school
and very carefully
avoid all the cracks
and lines in the pavement,
you'll be late.

David Horner

Pippa Said

My sister Pippa said:
'You should
never let a mirror break
never wear green shoes
never see one magpie
never squash a worm.
That's bad luck.'

And Jack said,
'Right.'

My sister Pippa said:
'You should
always catch a falling leaf
always knock on wood
always throw the salt you've spilt
always pick up pins.
That's good luck.'

And Jack said,
'Right.'

My sister Pippa said:
'You should
never sleep in the moonlight
never step on cracks
never put shoes on the table . . .'

And Jack said:
'You what? That's rubbish, that is!'
And he put his trainers on the table,
and Mum came in
and yelled at him.

And Pippa said:
'Told you!'

Jennifer Curry

Cracks in the Pavement

Those cracks in the pavement,
as everyone knows,
mustn't be stepped on.
Not even a toe
should venture to try it.
Don't laugh, it's quite true.
Let me tell you the story
of Brian McGrew,
who jumped on a crack
with an 'I don't care' grin.
At once, the crack opened.
The boy was dragged in
by a large, scaly hand.
He had time for one shriek,
then vanished entirely.
Gone for a week,
he was found in Australia,
mad as a hatter.
So don't say that avoiding
the cracks doesn't matter.
Just hop, skip and jump,
that's all you need do
while remembering the story
of Brian McGrew.

Marian Swinger

Foo

If people say,
'Bats bring bad tidings,' you
should quietly,
politely, tell them, 'Foo.'

For a bat, in Chinese,
is known as 'Foo'
and 'Foo' is Chinese
for happiness too.

'Foo!'

Mike Johnson

Kisses for Luck

Mum kissed her Premium Bonds
As she put them safely away.
Dad kissed his pools coupon
As he posted it yesterday.
I kissed my lottery ticket –
I hope to be over the moon.
With good luck from all that kissing
We'll surely be millionaires soon.

Eric Finney

The Thirteenth

We're a biggish family:
there's John and Emma, Kev and Lee,
Jemima, Sue, Hermione,
Harry, Barry, Titch and me.
That's eleven. Then there's Heidi.
We should call the next one Friday.

Jill Townsend

Touch Wood

I haven't had an accident all year,
During spring, summer, autumn or winter.
Hope my good fortune continues, touch wood.

Yow!

Got a splinter!

John Caulton

Fall Guy

'Don't walk under ladders –
It's UNLUCKY!' they say.
So if ever I see one –
I take it away . . .

And once I've removed it
They always agree
The guy who's climbed up
Is LESS LUCKY than me . . . !

Trevor Harvey

Good Luck

I found a lucky four-leaved clover
Growing on a wall.
I climbed for it and slipped and, ouch!
Cracked three ribs in my fall.
Thank goodness for the clover
Or I might have cracked them all.

Richard Edwards

64

On Reflection

I've broken my mirror!
How bad can things get?
For seven long years
I'll be sorry – and yet

My face is as ugly
As ugly can be,
And I've broken my mirror!
Well, LUCKY OLD ME.

Clare Bevan

You'll Stay Like That If the Wind Changes

I was pulling tongues at my sister
When the wind just suddenly changed.
Now I look like a Picasso
With my face bits all rearranged.

Jason Hulme

Bathroom Beliefs for Girls

Left foot first into the bath
  And you'll marry a man to make you laugh

Comb your hair before it's dry
  And you'll marry a man to make you sigh

Forget to dry between your toes
  And you'll marry a man with a runny nose

Wash your face without the soap
  And you'll marry a man who'll be a dope

Forget to rinse around the sink
  And you'll marry a man whose armpits stink

Brush your teeth before you wash
  And you'll marry a man who's awfully posh

Never wash or keep yourself clean
  And you'll marry . . . no one.
                        You know what I mean.

John Coldwell

What a Catch

Watch out,
Get ready,
Hands in the air,
Who will catch the bouquet?
Will it be Ellie, or Jennifer-Jane,
Or Chloe, or Anna, or Faye?

What strength,
What a throw,
See how the flowers go
Over the wedding marquee.
Great-Granny jumps up and calls out with glee,
'The next down the aisle is *me*!'

Cynthia Rider

An Unfortunate Mistake

I threw some rice at a wedding,
I threw it to bring good luck.
So why did everyone grumble?
And why did everyone duck?

I threw some rice at a wedding,
The vicar punched my chin!
And all because I used the sort
That's packed inside a tin.

Clare Bevan

Rosemary

'Why's Rosemary standing in a pot
outside the front door, Mum?
It's Halloween! It's trick or treat!
She should be having fun!'

'Rosemary's our protection, son,
on this most evil night.
I've read it in this book of lore,
she'll give the spooks a fright.'

'Is this the book you mean, Mum?'
'Yes, turn to chapter four . . .
to keep out wicked witches,
plant Rosemary at the door.'

Catharine Boddy

Digging Up Trouble

Gran said you can find buried treasure
where rainbows come down to the ground.
My brother's been digging for ages and ages,
and nothing but trouble he's found.

Dad's livid!
He says, when he finds him,
he'll wish he had never been born.
This rainbow appeared in the spray from the hose
and he's dug a great hole in the lawn.

Barry Buckingham

Saying Goodnight

Sharing a room with a sister,
Who's older and thinks she has rights,
Isn't easy when rights are unequal,
And she has control of the lights.

Because she was born first she chooses
If we should talk, read or fight,
But I won't go to sleep till I know that I've been
The last one to whisper *Goodnight*.

No I won't go to sleep till I know that I've been
The last one to whisper *Goodnight*.

It starts when she switches the light off,
And calls out *Goodnight*. I reply.
Each of knows that we *must* say it last,
Though neither really knows why.

The *Goodnights* fly to the ceiling,
They bounce quickly down to the floor.
For at least half an hour the *Goodnights* come and go,
Passing bookcase and wardrobe and door.

I wait till she thinks that I'm sleeping,
Till she thinks that her victory's complete,
Then I whisper *Goodnight*, and the real truth is known
By the darkness and me and the sheet.

Yes I whisper *Goodnight*, and the real truth is known
By the darkness and me and the sheet.

Daphne Kitching

I Also Have to Get Down the Stairs Before the Flush Stops

Happen you might have to read this poem again

Sometimes I have to
do everything twice sometimes
I have to do everything twice and
and if I'm walking past railings
I have to if I'm walking
past railings I have to touch them all

touch them all or I must
go back to the beginning or I must go
back to the beginning and start and start all over
all over once more

once more or something might happen

you might have to read this poem again
or something might

Dave Reeves

I'm much better now . . . touch wood!

I used to be superstitious –
carried a rabbit's foot,
wore a crowded charm bracelet,
nothing but red,
and, outside school,
always my lucky baseball cap.

When I say I was superstitious
my condition was so serious
I had corns on my knuckles
from the constant wood-knocking,
and my crossing-fingers
were becoming double helical!

Since then I've had therapy.
Nowadays I carry only a rabbit's toe,
three charms on my bracelet
and confine my wearing of red
to socks and underwear –
also I knock on wood no more than once a week.

Although my schoolwork hasn't improved
(Why won't they let me wear my lucky cap?)
my therapist says I've done so well
she's downgraded
my condition to stitious.
Stitious, wow! Isn't that super!

Philip Waddell

How to Survive School

Poems chosen by

David Harmer

Forget textbooks or calculators, <u>HERE</u> is the essential item you need to survive school!

Discover the best way to deal with every school occasion. Learn how to outwit the dinner lady and befriend the caretaker, how to divert attention from yourself and appear to be paying attention and how to win the best part in the school play.

My Best Subject

I'm no good at history, rubbish at maths
And geography, and all the rest;
But at blackmailing teachers I'm really quite good,
So I always do well in the tests.

Rob Falconer

How to Embarrass Teachers

Poems chosen by Paul Cookson

It's time to get even with your teachers!

Ever cringed at something your teacher has said or done? Then these poems are for you!

Now's the time to find out how a well-placed whoopee cushion (among other things) can make your teacher squirm . . .

Biting Mad

I love to make my teacher mad,
I love to make him shout
cos when his tongue gets tangled up
his new false teeth fall out!

Celia Gentles

CAN WE HAVE OUR BALL BACK, PLEASE?

Football poems by Gareth Owen

A truly top-of-the-league collection of football poems!

Gareth Owen's lifelong love of football blazes through this stunning book of beautifully crafted poems. All the joy, sorrow and sheer fun of being a player and a fan can be found in this wonderfully funny and heartwarming collection.

Can We Have Our Ball Back, Please?

England gave football to the world
Who, now they've got the knack,
Play it better than we do
And won't let us have it back.

A selected list of titles available from Macmillan Children's Books

---

How to Survive School

Poems chosen by David Harmer   978-0-330-43951-0   £3.99

How to Embarrass Teachers

Poems chosen by Paul Cookson   978-0-330-44276-3   £3.99

Can We Have Our Ball Back, Please?

Football poems by Gareth Owen   978-0-330-44048-6   £3.99
